**Let's Not be Afraid Stories**

as told by Alperas, son of Anubis,
and Marian Wenzel

Stories for Children and Grown-ups

# Let's Not be Afraid Stories

as told by Alperas, son of Anubis,
and Marian Wenzel

Stories for Children and Grown-ups

*Illustrated by the authors*

Blue Dragon Press

To Azra Begić
who gave Anubis to John


© Marian Wenzel

First published in 1996 by
Blue Dragon Press Limited
2 Holly House, Rose Hill
Dorking, Surrey RH4 2EQ (UK)

All rights reserved

Illustrations by Marian Wenzel
Design and typesetting by Aztec Design, Guildford, Surrey (UK)
Printed by GOPrint, Guildford, Surrey (UK)


No part of this book may be reproduced or transmitted in any form or by any means, electronic or mechanical, including photocopying, recording, or by any information storage, transmission and retrieval system, without written permission from the publisher.

British Library Catalogue-in-Publication Data
A Catalogue record for this book is available from the British Library


ISBN 1 900 36507 3

# Introduction

Anubis, father of Alperas who is the talented, jackal-headed author of the stories in this book, entered the home of Marian and John in 1986. In the Spring of that year, Marian visited Sarajevo and returned with a gift for John from a friend there – an ancient wooden statue of Anubis from Egypt. The upright, jackal-headed figure had one remaining arm which moved on a pin. Marian and John learned this arm could be stood upright when John needed particular help. Soon after the arrival of the statue, Marian's hand began to move of itself, and she received the automatic writing introducing Anubis and his family, and setting out the stories by Alperas which are related here.

Alperas was first presented to John by Anubis as a motherless orphan, who needed to be John's stepson, and receive his care. The mother of Alperas had been a beautiful desert jackal, with whom Anubis was in love, who got killed. Yet she soon re-emerged in the home of Marian and John (after thousands of years of course), as the lovely spirit-jackal Asteras, and had three more jackal-headed children – Stella Marian, John Arlesis and Stella Sothis. The names of Marian and John were incorporated into the names of the first two children who were born in their house, as a sign of respect.

On April 25, 1988, Marian's notes say that John did some thinking about the names of Anubis' "furry family", over lunch. He told Marian, he had read in a book that the Virgin Mary could be called Stella Maris, which sounded a lot the same as "Stella Marian", daughter of Anubis. "Marian" was a form of the Hebrew name "Miryam", the Virgin Mary's name, meaning a droplet of the sea. So Stella Marian's name meant something like "star of the sea". That was a single star, but the name of Anubis' wife, the spirit-jackal "Asteras", related to names for the whole starry heavens, resembling the word "astral" or else the name for a personification of the Milky Way, "Asterios".

But he really was just guessing what those names meant. And he had no idea what "Alperas" meant.

Anubis said, '"Alperas" is the name of the dog acting as keeper of going to look at temples in Egypt on the part of tourist agencies, and he's the uncle of this Alperas. But he's much too busy to come to England'.

John then told Anubis, he had been reading a book he liked, *Egyptian Gods and Goddesses*, but couldn't find any family of Anubis there. Anubis said, his family wasn't known. It was private to him, and he'd been able to keep them out of books this way. Once Egyptian gods became known, they were made to work very hard, and Anubis did not approve of child labour. When Alperas wrote stories, that was not work. That was *education*, for John helped him with his English.

With the birth of more children to Anubis, Alperas grew to be older and developed into an author. He got a big book and began to write stories into it, which he read to John, whenever John needed to laugh. Sometimes he read the stories to his new brother and sisters, but basically they were for John.

On October 30, 1988, Anubis told John that Asteras was about to give birth in about two weeks to a second little girl, who was to be called "Stella Sothis". She would also be jackal-headed, like everyone else in the immediate family, except for one uncle, Saperas, who was of real jackal shape, like his sister, Asteras. Non-blood uncles – such as Thoth and Apis – looked like standard creatures, in this case, ibis and bull.

John looked up at "Sothis" in *Egyptian Gods and Goddesses* and found the name. Sothis was the Egyptian goddess that was the same as Sirius, the Dog Star. She was always shown with a star on the top of her head. John said, those star images were originally Babylonian, so there might be some Babylonian qualities about Anubis' family. Maybe writing good stories would be one.

*February 3, 1987*
*This Alperas writes to John.*
'Dear John. It's Alperas. And the story I'm telling now is told by the new means: I let my little brother take little boxes he doesn't know what they have in them. Each box has the picture of something in it. Like Baldwin the coot. Whatever is on the picture in the box he picks out, has to be in the story.'

'This time he chose two things. The picture of Baldwin, and then a little green man. So the story has to be about Baldwin the coot and a green man.'

'Last time you heard about Talky Taylor and the little green men. They put their space ship on that umbrella-shaped yew outside his door, that looks like a support made for one, and he got taken prisoner. You remember that. In the end they stole just his wine cellar. These are the same little green men, only just one is there.'

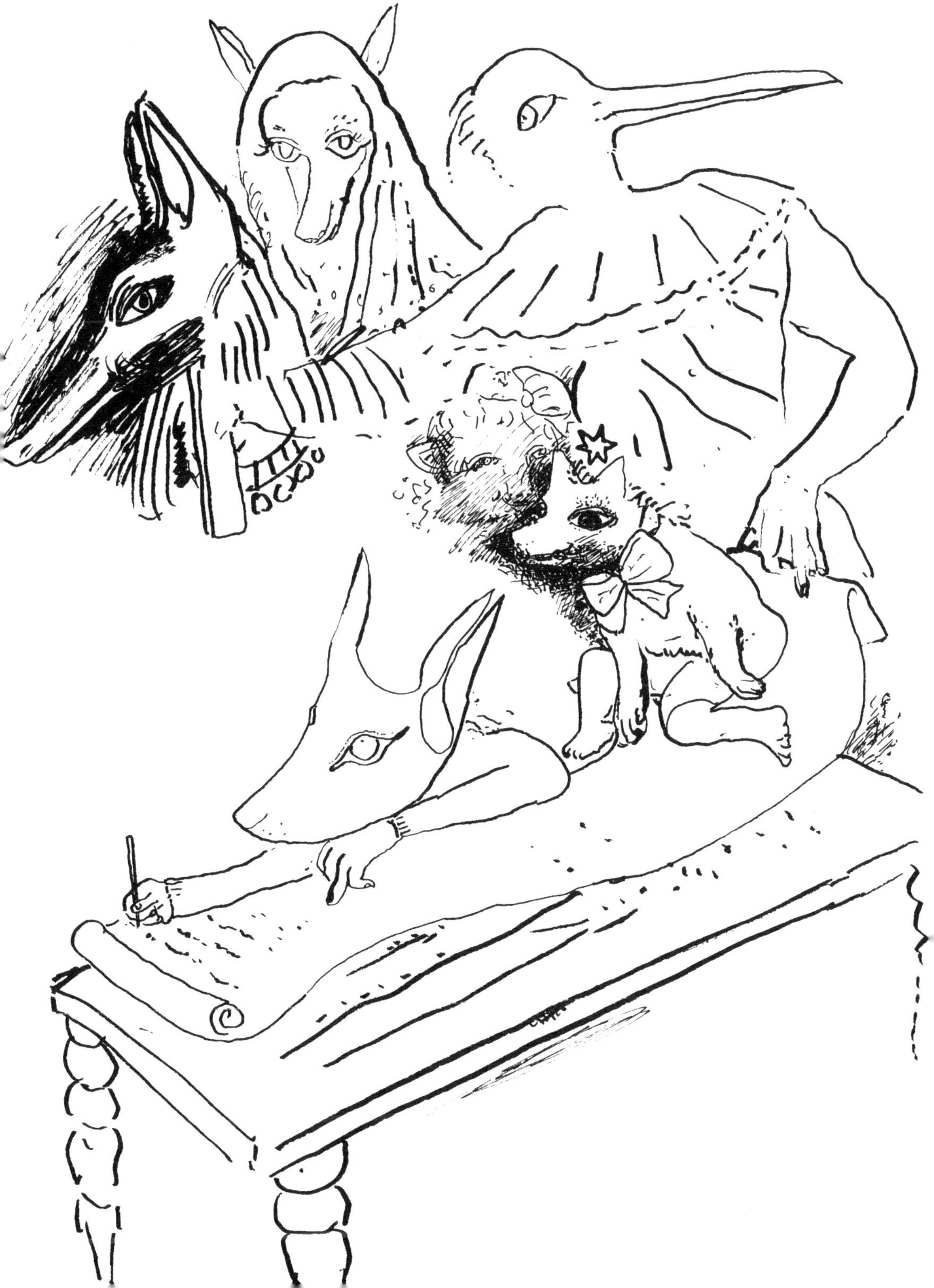

# 1 • Baldwin the Coot and a Little Green Man

Baldwin blew on his feathers. He liked blowing on his feathers because they looked lots prettier and lady coots liked him more. Suddenly, a little green man put his head up right next to Baldwin in the water and said, 'COR, YOU LOOK SEXY.' Baldwin is dignified and he felt not a little aggrieved at this.

'I don't want to look sexy to you,' he said huffily.

'Maybe you don't, but you do,' said the little green man, who had big goggle eyes Baldwin found not very nice.

'Pity you can't go somewhere else,' said Baldwin.

'Isn't it? But I can't,' said the green man, 'I've got my spaceship moored just nearby.'

'Might be nice if you took off,' said Baldwin.

'Tell me,' said the little green man. 'Tonight we need some entertainment. If we provided the wine, how would you waterfowl like to…'

'Provide the waterfowl?' said Baldwin testily. 'No thanks. Nobody eats coot around me. And certainly not utilizing me, or any of my friends.'

At this point Baldwin steamed up the millstream like some kind of tornado. The little green man turned to avoid him but got clawed right in his horrible goggle eye.

He watched what he said to coots after that.

*Alperas*

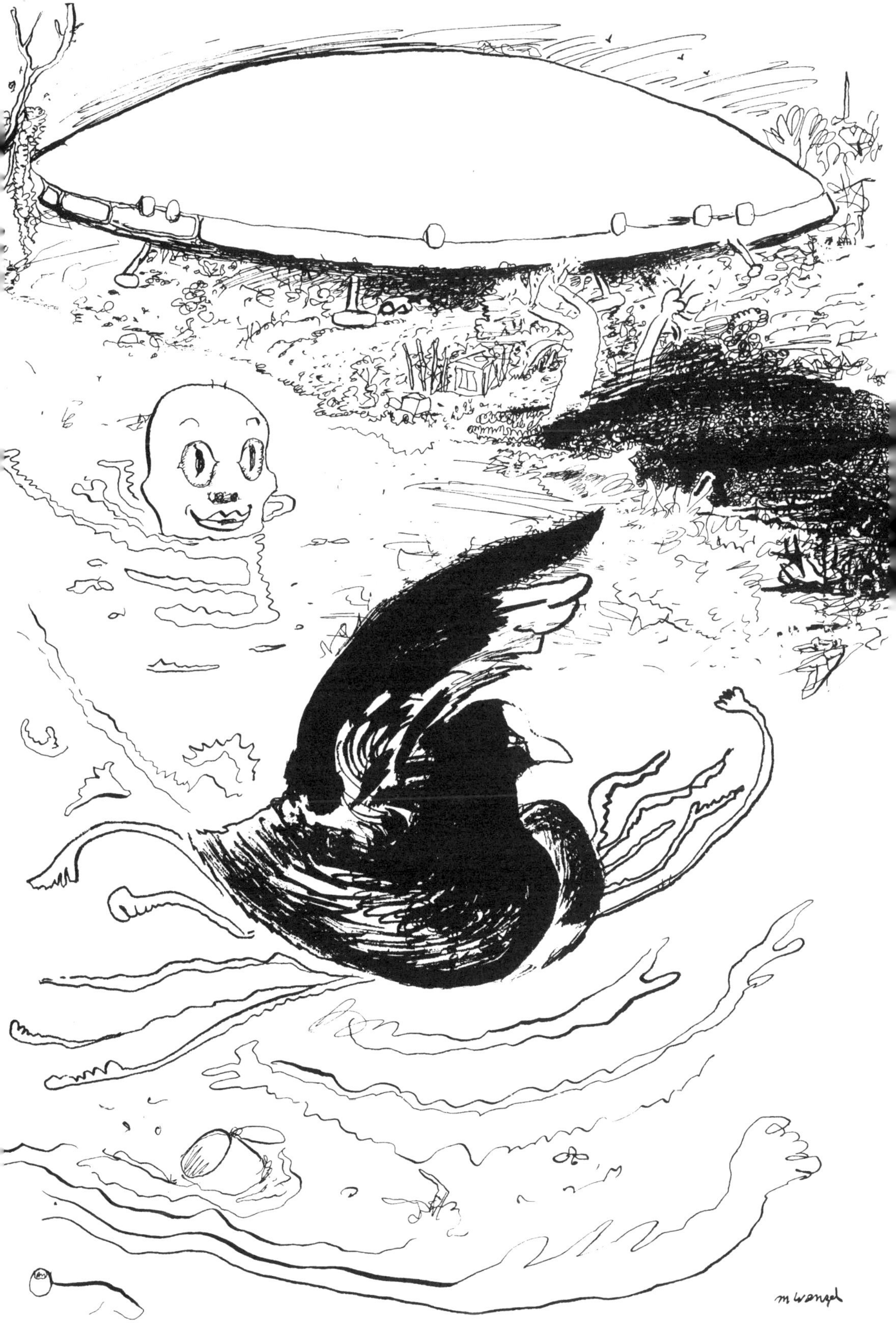
m wenzel

*December 24, 1987*

## 2 • A Christmas Story from Alperas to John

Who hears a story now about three loose pigs trying to be eternally free and leaders of other pigs in danger of being cooked.

Once three pigs were born at one time. They got born with striped stockings. That made them look pretty peculiar. The farmer that owned them was sure the other farmers in his farming association would find out and think he had contaminated their feed. He thought he must get rid of these pigs.

The three pigs hoped they got a chance to look more closely at his plate of Christmas dinner. They feared he ate pig. They had a good look at his food, pretending to be silverware on the table, and saw he did eat pig. They feared for lives of all pigs they knew. So they decided to go round on Christmas Eve when he was off his work, and brand stockings on the legs of all the other pigs they liked. They did. The farmer thought all the pigs were ruined. He got his big gun and decided to shoot them all.

The three pigs let him take the gun. Then they let him get ready to shoot, and butted him from behind. He shot himself. Then they set all the pigs free and started a community. They were the business managers.

*Alperas*

A drawing is inserted here, of Alperas clutching something, and beside it: 'That's me with stories I ripped up. I keep only the nicest for John.'

*Alperas*

# 3 • Mermaids, Green Men and Jackson the Seal

Here is the story of a famous seal, called Jackson. He was a misogynist. He lived on an island with a lot of other seals and fourteen mermaids. The mermaids liked mirrors, fish and marooned sailors, but these days they got hardly any of the first and last.

Because Jackson was a lot cleverer than the other seals, he taught school. Once everyone heard a crunching sound and it was a ship getting aground. It was not the usual sort of ship; it was a spaceship. Little green men came out and captured the mermaids, as hostages. They were put in a tank. They called for help.

Jackson never admitted it, but he liked the mermaids really. He put up his flipper and set off an alarm in the police station where there were eagles. They came at once and forced entry in to the spaceship and rescued the mermaids, although some eagles got killed. The mermaids were very grateful and said to Jackson, 'You can marry us if you want, even if you are only a seal.'

Jackson said, 'Thank you very much, I don't want to.'

*A story by Alperas.*


*June 7, 1988*

# 4 • Miss Brody and the Dragon

Alperas designed a story that was so frightening, Marian would not fall asleep in the middle. It involved a local shop-mistress, Miss Brody, an ex-school-mistress with a fondness for Wimbledon, who was interrupted reading a pornographic magazine on her birthday by a dragon at the front door, who knocked. He said he had a "dragonogram" for her.

The dragon's "dragonogram" meant, he carried her off to a desert where there were diamonds around but not much else. She looked like going to be stuck there, so she blew a whistle she had, and from the horizon on all sides came witches riding ironing boards. They were from the kind of ladies club she was in — each had a whistle to call the others. They threatened the dragon with pulling out his scales one by one. So the dragon took her home.

*A story by Alperas.*

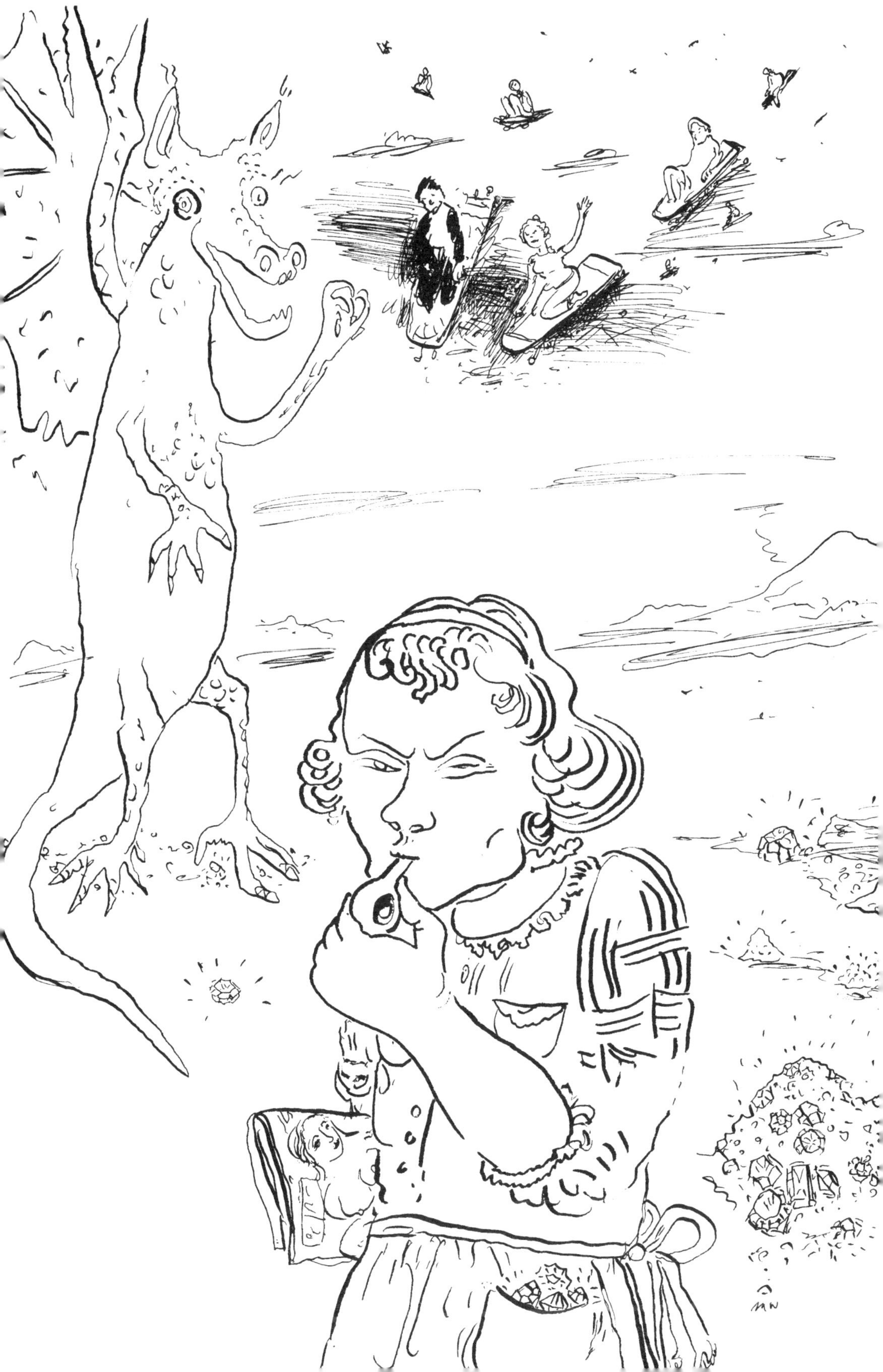

# 5 • Three Frogs

This story is about three frogs. They lived in the house where the local pub character, "Talky" Taylor used to live, which was now sold. They were each a little bigger than the last, and had puffy faces. They happened to be on the mantelpiece of a room in which the new mistress of the house was giving a party. Someone admired her "china" frogs, but when she looked at them, she saw they were real. She didn't make any remark as she didn't want to shock the guests and the frogs sat very quietly not moving a muscle.

But when the guests had gone she said, 'Now you get out.'

The frogs didn't want to go, they liked it there. But she said something threatening like, 'You'd better go while you still can.'

So the frogs went out, and hopped away 'till they came to an open field. There they stopped, saying to each other, 'It's better to live somewhere less grand, than somewhere grand where people can come along and throw you out.'


*Monday, October 24, 1988.*

Thoth had a birthday. He was going to Egypt to his temple outside Karnak to receive homage from all the Pharaohs. There was a drawing made by Alperas of how he would look receiving the homage.

Meanwhile, Alperas had got in to trouble because Anubis and Thoth felt he had become over-helpful with some theatre music John was writing, leading it to become bogged down. They decided Alperas could be allowed to help John with woodworking, but not with music. John begged them to let him still be allowed, but Anubis was firm. So Alperas wrote a letter to John and left it where he would find it.

The letter was a drawing (see illustration). Its caption said, 'Alperas puts an ibis mask on a pole and acts being Thoth.'

'Dear John,' says the shaky-voiced god. 'Alperas is the best little boy to help you in the whole world!'

John made a birthday supper for Thoth of some meat which was slow-cooked in Guinness with mushrooms and onions and leeks. There was a red chenille cloth with green mats on it and a red candle that Alperas was allowed to light. And the clocks got put back. Alperas was allowed to do that job too.

Alperas
puts an ibis mask
on a pole
and acts being
THOTH
Dear John says the shaky-voiced god
Alperas is the best little boy
to help you in the WHOLE WORLD
m wenzel

*October 26, 1988*

## 6 • The Seven Flies

Alperas told a story about seven flies. They were in the house as Autumn came, and told each other they should Winter there. But one of them, noticing several other flies lying on their backs dead on the window sills, said that was no place for them; they should leave and be outside.

The one wary fly managed to get out, and he flew and flew, and came to a ship which he entered, that took him to Africa where it was warm and there were a lot of other flies and he lived happily ever after.

The others all died.

*A story by Alperas.*

♥♥♥♥♥♥♥

*Alperas says, this story is important because it shows you how life is saved by looking at changed circumstances and letting them be your guide to action.*

## 7 • The Jackal-Headed Boy and Superman

After dinner, John was told he would get a short story from Alperas, to top all the others. It was about getting to be Superman. A jackal-headed boy made a superman costume, put it on, and went out and met a man.

'I'm Superman,' he said to the man. The man said, 'You're a super silly dog.'

The boy then decided he would have more effect as Superman if he approached people backwards. He went backwards, but he got a stick to hold out his cloak so it looked as if he were rushing the other direction, and it was flying out behind him.

He met a little girl.

'I'm Superman,' he said. She said, 'I think you look like a fire engine.'

The little jackal-headed boy began to think he wasn't much success as Superman. He looked up, however, and saw a dot in the sky, getting bigger and bigger. It was Superman. He came right down to him and said, 'How's my favourite incarnation?' He then picked up the little boy and flew away with him into the clouds.

m Wenzel

## 8 • The Two Mud-puddles

One night, John wasn't getting to sleep and kept talking. Alperas told John he'd tell him a story to help him get to sleep. He warned him it was a dirty story. It was about two mud puddles.

One mud puddle said to the other, 'Let's dry up.' So they did.

John said that sounded like American jokes. But Anubis broke in and said, that was wrong. The story let John know the decision to be quiet was his. He didn't have to be keeping Marian awake. In case he forgot he had the power to be quiet, Alperas reminded him he did.

*February 13, 1989*
*Anubis said there was news. Alperas had become a Boy Scout. He had a Boy Scout uniform Asteras had made and he went to meetings in a local Worcester school. This led Alperas to compose some new stories, about Boy Scouts.*

## 9 • Two Scouts and a Snake

A Boy Scout and a Brownie Scout were walking along. The Boy Scout was protecting the Brownie Scout because it was one of his Good Deeds. As they went along they met a snake, right across the path, obstructing their way. Suddenly it stood up, all the way on the end of its tail, and said, 'I am Shiva.' 'Good,' said the Boy Scout. 'Now we can get by.'

*A story by Alperas.*

♥♥♥♥♥♥♥

*John didn't like that story too well, and Alperas got hurt. So John said, it wasn't that he didn't like it really, he just thought it was odd. Then Alperas said, he had made it up to point out, good Boy Scouts get on with the tasks they have decided to do and don't waste time being surprised.*

## 10 • The Boy Scouts that were Green Men

Two green men from outer space wanted to be Boy Scouts. They had boy-costumes so no-one could tell them from boys, and they went and sat in the Boy Scout meetings. They were called Mick and Jack.

In the Scout meetings they learned how they were supposed to do Good Deeds. They decided to go up in their spaceship, and spot out deeds to do. They went up and saw a little old lady unable to cross the street. They came down in the street to help her, and the traffic all stopped, but the little old lady fled in the opposite direction.

Then they noticed a dog swimming across a stream in danger of drowning. They went to rescue the dog, but when it saw them it went in to a fit, and they had to give it tranquilizing shots to do anything for it at all.

Then they had to go to another Boy Scout meeting so they put on their boy disguises. On the way to the meeting they met an old lady trying to cross the road. They said could they help her, and she said certainly, she was very happy to have their help. So they helped her. Then they saw a dog of failing strength in the middle of swimming a stream. They just whistled on the bank, like boys do, and this gave him the courage to swim the rest of the way. So they decided to be boys from then on. And then they were.

*A story by Alperas.*

♥♥♥♥♥♥♥

*Alperas said about that story, helping others works best if you try to be like the people you help.*

## 11 • The Scout and the Birds

This story is about a single Boy Scout. He started being followed by hundreds and hundreds of birds. They begged him to do a Good Deed for them. They all had pale coloured beaks, and this attracted a lot of attention. For instance, their children were caught by predators because their white beaks showed up too much. They begged the boy scout to do the Good Deed of painting their beaks dark.

The Boy Scout said, they would have to get Darwin to be a Boy Scout and do evolution all over again, to make the beaks dark. He couldn't do it. And he turned his back on the birds and went in the other direction.

*A story by Alperas.*

♥♥♥♥♥♥♥

*Alperas said, Scouts have to know the difference between doing Good Deeds and being exploited to carry out silly jobs.*


October 31, 1988

*Alperas told a story at breakfast called:*
## 12 • Alperas' Wonderful Story of the Week

Once there were two firebirds. They lived in Georgia, in the Caucasus, in a mountain plain. Their wings were long and curled, like flames, and smoke rose from the end of each feather. The feathers on their breasts were small green and blue flames. The two of them were exactly like each other (as these birds are) except the male bird had a crest.

A boy who rode his horse every day in to that part of the mountains to follow sheep was keeping close watch on them. They had a nest high in a tree in a secret rocky place he knew. He used to look at them for hours, creeping up to an overhanging rock on a nearby pinnacle, where another rock shielded him from view from the parent firebirds who flew over him to tend the nest.

One day the baby firebird was born. It was like a little ball of fire. Its beak was like steel, and the end of its fluffy feathers sparkled like a sparkler, with the sparks like stolen diamonds.

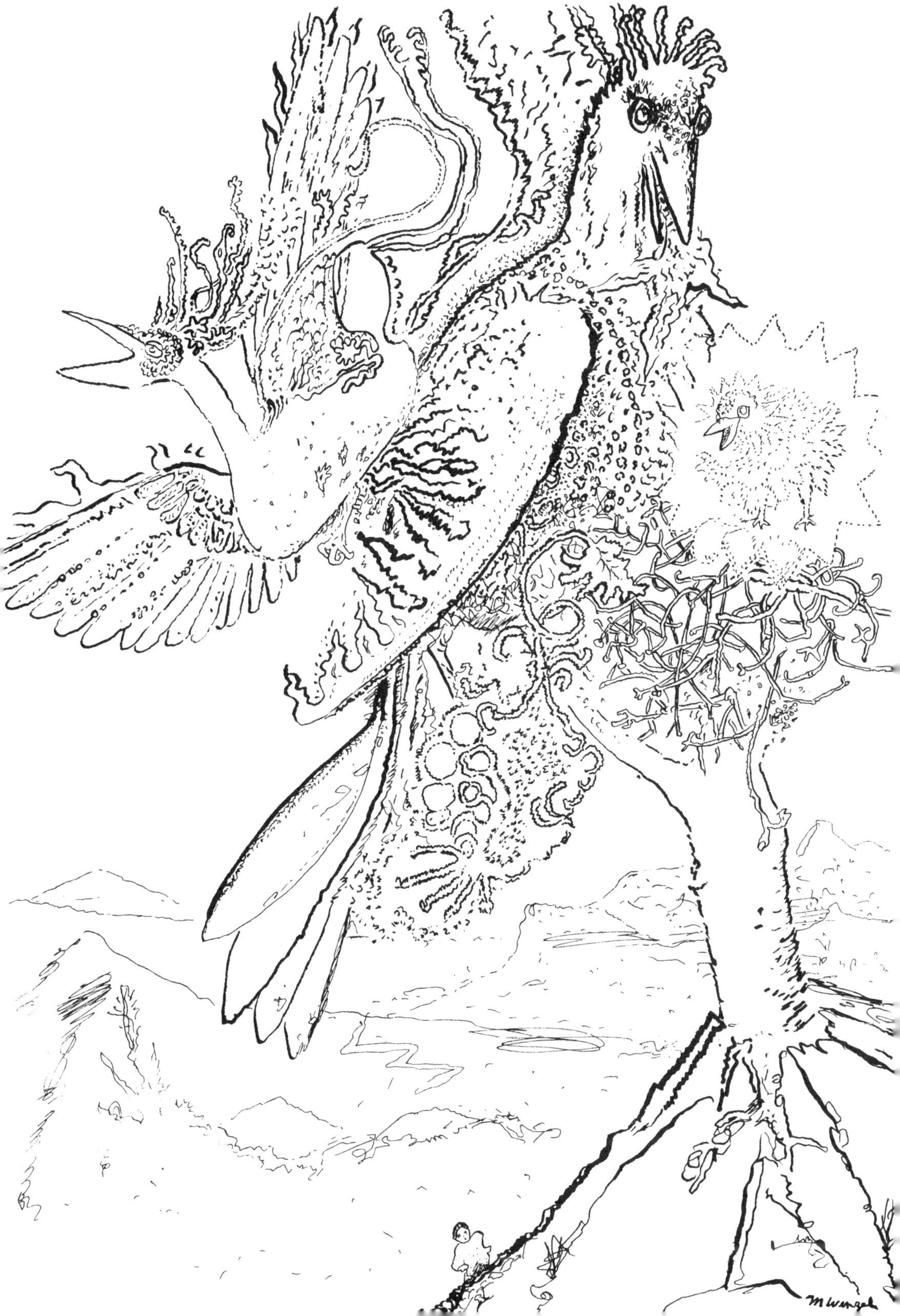

The boy wanted the little firebird badly. He decided to catch it in a net. He didn't think anything about how he would feed it once he had got it. He only wanted to have it.

He constructed the net of thick cord, which he made fireproof. When he went up to the place where the nest was with his net, the parent firebirds by chance were not there. He climbed the tree and hurled the net over the baby firebird, and caught it.

At once the parent firebirds appeared. They beat him with their fiery wings. But he slid down the tree and ran, clutching the netted chick. Then he fell over a rock. The net sprang open and the baby firebird flew out of it, as if it had always known how to fly, right back in to the nest. The parent firebirds left the boy alone and went off to tend it.

But when the boy stood up, he found he was completely different. Because he was now someone who had netted a firebird. It didn't matter if he didn't keep it. He had netted it. And that was what mattered. Now he could do anything.

*A story by Alperas.*

♥♥♥♥♥♥♥

*Anubis said, this story had been told to John (who was still having trouble writing his music) to let him know he could do anything, because he had netted the Furry Family.*

*November 5, 1988*

## 13 • The Firecracker

This story is short, because Alperas lost the original and hopes he finds it. He doesn't want to change it new ways when he reads it out now, because he likes best how he had it first.

The firecracker who is hero of this story was very brave, and had the courage to be a firecracker twice. He was brought out with other firecrackers when he came out the first time, but stopped himself being sent in to the air by the complicated series of events which Alperas doesn't quite remember, and doesn't want to tell wrong.

The second time the firecracker was brought out, it decided not to mind ending up blazing. But instead, to enjoy the ride in the sky.

*A story by Alperas.*

♥♥♥♥♥♥♥

*John thought that story was about death. But Alperas said, of course not. "Hesitating to get into action" was the story's theme. You can miss out once. But then, by tiny totally insignificant steps you can get to be a firecracker a second time. You can be better the second time, because you have thought what you want, and the bottom of the heavens becomes your path through the sky! This is real fun! And when you leave the sky, it's because you are old and worn out and genuinely want to stop.*

*November 21, 1988*

In the night, Anubis' second daughter, Stella Sothis, was born to his jackal wife, Asteras. She was all furry and white, like a puppy, with a star of pearls on her forehead. She soon turned into a baby with a fuzzy white dog's head, and the star still in place.

Alperas was still helping John when the birth happened, and told him. John also learned that some amateur slides of temples in Tibet a friend of Marian's had been showing her that evening, and a gift by the same friend of a baby-size blanket from Nepal, were also appropriate for the Stella Sothis birth.

Even the phrases "How wonderful", which Marian had bored John with by saying as each slide was shown, and "It's a moonscape", which her guest had bored him by saying at the same time, were appropriate.

## 14 • The Little Sting-ray

Alperas told a story which he said was exciting from the very beginning. It took place in the ocean.

A daddy sting-ray was explaining to his son, who was busy eating a sort of grub, how the sting-ray was dangerous. The little sting-ray asked, 'What is dangerous?'

Daddy sting-ray explained, it meant if he met something living he didn't like, he could put out these rays, and he could kill it.

The little sting-ray asked, 'What is killing?' Daddy said, 'Like you're doing to that grub.'

The little sting-ray asked, 'Can I do it to you?'

Daddy sting-ray said no he couldn't, because they were the same. It had to be something different.

Then daddy sting-ray went off, and along came a mermaid. She was tall and stood on the tip of her tail, and was ever so beautiful. She had goggle-blue eyes, and glittering diamonds everywhere. She said to the little sting-ray,

'You're nice. I think you'd make a nice bow for my hair.'

The little sting-ray said, 'I'm dangerous. I can harm people. I just learned.'

The mermaid said, 'Fine. Then you can protect me,' and took him and put him in her hair.

*A story by Alperas.*

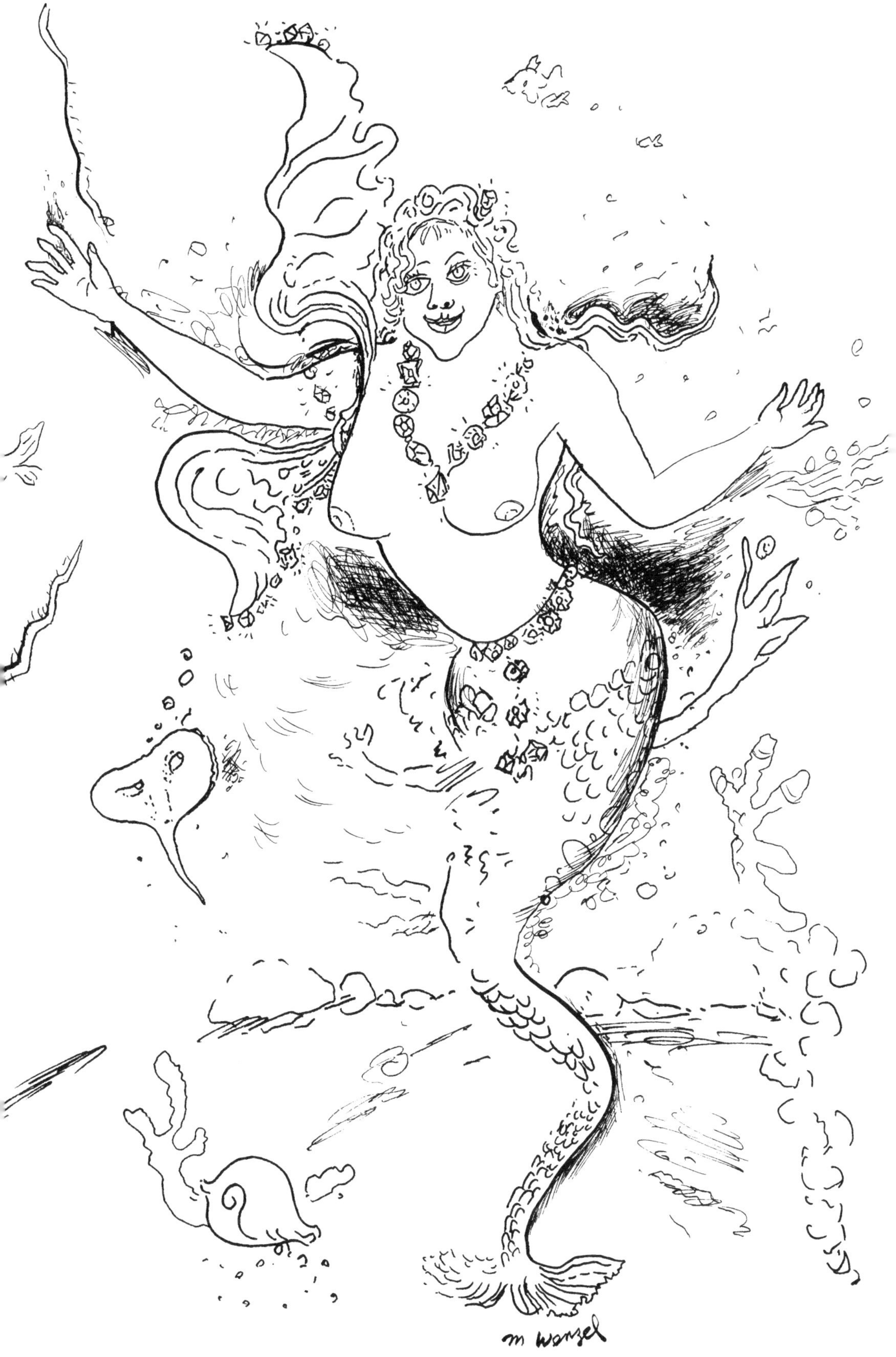
m wenzel

*November 28, 1988*

## 15 • The Boy at School

In the morning, Alperas told a story about a little boy at school. It showed how a philosophical concept turned into real boys.

The boy at school hated school, but liked being best. He had lots of success in philosophy and mathematics. He liked symbolic logic and particularly, truth tables. He took an interest in them particularly.

He said, 'There are two statements. One is True and one is Not True. It is True I know they are True and Not True. The best part is, they are True. So they are little boys like me, called True and Not True.'

Then they all quit school and went fishing.

*A story by Alperas.*


*January 9, 1989*
*John and Marian had read in an encyclopedia about birds, that English coots could migrate to Germany. This seemed strange. They had noticed ducks and swans in flight, but not coots. The local coots got excited, and flew at each other sometimes, but that looked to be all they did in the flying line.*
*Alperas had this to say:*

## 16 • Flight of the Coots

A lot of waterbirds lived together on still water near some old buildings on an inland river tributary. There were lots of ducks, six geese, some moorhens and two coots. One day there came to the water, some Canada geese. They told these coots they had often met others like them, winging their way to Germany. 'Do we do that?' asked the coots, looking startled. They never thought they did that. The Canada geese said of course, they saw them often. They thought all coots did that.

The coots were ashamed, and talked among themselves, and decided they would fly to Germany. So they set off. But they had not flown long when their wings began to get tired. They were only at a village, but not far from where they had been before. 'Is this Germany?' asked the lady coot. The male coot said maybe it was, and anyway, it was time to go back now. So back they went.

'What, back already?' asked the Canada geese. 'Where did you go?'

'We went to Germany,' said the coots.

'Certainly not,' said the Canada geese. 'It takes a much, much longer time than that.'

The coots were embarrassed, and decided to set out once more. They flew and flew. They were nearly exhausted. Finally they came to a great grey expanse of water, that stretched on and on.

'Where is this? Is this Germany?' asked the lady coot.

'No,' said the male. 'But I don't want you flying over this water when you are tired. We are going back.'

When the coots got back, the Canada geese were gone. 'Where have you been?' asked the other birds.

'Germany,' said the coots.

*A story by Alperas.*

## 17 • Coots on Noah's Ark

Two coots were on Noah's Ark. They were beautifully brightened by feathers of all tones. The horrible truth they learned was: Noah — and quite possibly God — liked birds best that were black and white. Noah chose first the raven and then the dove to go forth and seek land. The coots felt they were better able to serve — they carried sticks well, and flew well. For instance, books existed recording how coots flew to Germany. So the coots decided to be just black and white. And so they were.

*A story by Alperas, who says, this story means, you can be what you decide.*

# 18 • The Crocus that Angered Birds

This story was about the garden of Marian and John. A huge orange crocus grew up in it. Much larger than the bird bath, but not far from it. The birds were cross. They didn't like the crocus, because it got in their way, and it was much too big for them to eat, like they did with pansies and early primroses.

The birds told the crocus it was ugly. It was too big and grown in quite the wrong season. The crocus said it wasn't its fault, it just got that way. Suddenly a big truck drew up in the area outside the garden and parked. An Indian in a turban jumped out of the truck and ran into the garden. He bowed before the crocus, saying, 'O sacred Lotus, here I have found you where it was predicted you would be, I will take you back to my temple.' And he carefully removed the lotus and put it in his truck and took it away.

*A story by Alperas.*

♥ ♥ ♥ ♥ ♥ ♥ ♥

*Alperas says that story means that in doing nothing but accepting destiny, you can find yourself born out of season. Too tall. Too short. Bullied by those in your sphere. Then you learn you never belonged to that sphere. You belonged to being more special than that.*

Marian Wenzel

*March 9, 1989*

## 19 • The Ladybird and the Flower

Alperas so hurried to hunt for this story in the manuscript book of stories he wrote, that he spilled the honey soup he was having for breakfast. The story was dedicated to John, who had been cross with Marian. There were only two characters in it, a kind of bug called a ladybird, and a flower.
The flower was pink, with many blooms on one stem, and red edges to each bloom. It was Spring blooming, and it was called "Narcissus". Marian said, didn't he mean 'Hyacinth', and John got more annoyed, and said the flower was whatever Alperas said. Alperas said, well maybe hyacinth, but it bloomed in the Spring and was very beautiful.

The ladybird came and sat on it, and began walking over one of its leaves.

'Who's here?' said the flower. 'You are early.'

'I know,' said the ladybird. 'But I'd rather be early. I see lots of things the other ladybirds never get to see. For instance, I'd rather look at you than all the flowers of summer.'

The flower was flattered. She had no other such admirers. She said to the ladybird, 'You can stay on my leaves always and make them your home.'

But time passed, and the blooms on the flower turned brown round the edges and began to drop off. 'I'm afraid I'm wilting,' said the flower to the bug. 'You'd better go find yourself another flower. There are a lot of new ones about.'

'No,' said the ladybird. 'This is my home. I don't like you less because your blooms are brown. And I shall always remember you as you were.'

So the bug stayed on the flower forever.

*A story by Alperas.*

m Wenzel

*March 23, 1989*

## 20 • Ibis Humour

Walking to the Do-It-All shop, John thought of Thoth, and Thoth came. He told John, he had noticed John laughing at Alperas' stories. He said he would now be the one to tell John something funny. It was an example of Ibis Humour. It was this.

'John has three heads. Each is an ibis head. What's his position?'

John said he couldn't guess.

Thoth said, 'Lost in ibis eyes.'

John said it was of course awfully funny, but it was a bit mysterious.

Thoth looked satisfied. He said, that was what Ibis Humour was supposed to be.


*April 9, 1989*

## 21 • Two Squirrels

Two parent squirrels felt they were not good at anything, like John tended to say sometimes about himself, and certainly not up to being compared with the other beasts of the forest, in respect to their skills. They often spoke of it. They had a nest high in a tree — a hole in a tree branch. One day they found their baby squirrel was missing from it, and they blamed the fact they had often said they were not good at anything. They were being punished for their words. So the two squirrels set to recall all the things they did well. These included storing food for Winter, and keeping their children warm and fed when other animals starved.

Then suddenly they found the baby squirrel was not lost at all. He was hiding, near the mouth of their nest. And they learned, one more thing squirrels were good at, was hiding themselves.

*A story by Alperas.*

## *Alperas Stories and the Anubis News*
*July 31, 1989*

When Marian was met by John at Worcester Shrub Hill Station this time, they had a pizza and walked up the Shrub Hill to home. John remembered it was the day Alperas brought out the *Anubis News*. It was to feature, they had been told, the deeds of Anubis himself this week. They hurried up to the house, and found the newspaper waiting.

The main headline was: "ANUBIS NOTICES NO NEWS." And there was a big picture of him not noticing it. Then there was a headline, "ANUBIS ATTACKS SOFT PILLOWS." That was because little John Arlesis was under one, and they were having a tussle. Literature was a story written by Alperas himself, which was called "PREPARE TO MEET THY POPPY." Here it is.

## 22 • Prepare to Meet Thy Poppy

A poppy lived in a beautiful garden part way up a busy hill, transversed by little roads. Little yellow buses went up and down the hill like bumblebees, picking people up and letting them off. The poppy watched all this.

One day the poppy decided it would uproot itself, go down, and climb up the sides of one of the buses. It would tie itself to something on top of the bus, and call down in a human voice it would get, and greet all the people getting off and on. It thought about this, and knew — was sure — it could do all those things, but somehow it benignly decided, for the moment, not to do so.

Then there was a great event. Two people from far-away America, Eleanor and Niel (who came last week) arrived at the garden. By staying in the garden, the poppy was able to greet these people, who were more special than anyone it would have met going up and down the road in buses. So it decided to stay in place in the garden always.

*A story by Alperas.*

*September 9, 1989*
*While Marian and John were waiting on the platform for the Oxford-Didcot train, Alperas told another of the series of stories he made up concerning peacock pies. He felt there had not been enough real peacock pies in the book called that (by Walter De La Mare) that Marian had.*

## 23 • Peacock Igloo Pie

This story, Alperas said, begins with flashing lights. They are the Northern Lights. The story is about a peacock off course. The peacock belonged to a Maharajah in India and lived in a palace there. But he loved the sun. He thought the rising sun must be a great peacock, spreading its tail. And he decided if he flew through the night, he could come to where the peacock was, and watch him rise, and spread out his tail.

So he set out at twilight, flying north. He flew and flew. Finally he began to tire. And there were the Northern Lights, lighting what he saw. He looked down and saw a kind of mound, like a big pie, all of snow and ice. He thought that must be where the peacock lived. He flew down and entered it. It was an igloo. But where you would expect Eskimos, there was a giant peacock, about to leave the igloo and unfold his tail. He said,

'My child, you are tired. I am god of all peacocks. Mount on my back and take strength from my wings. For the spreading of my tail will give light to all the sky.'

The peacock did so. The giant peacock emerged from the pie-like igloo, and his tail lit up the whole sky. Day came, and they flew south, returning the peacock to the Maharajah's palace in India.

*A story by Alperas.*

♥ ♥ ♥ ♥ ♥ ♥ ♥

*Alperas said, this story was for people who hunted things in the wrong place. Dawn doesn't lie north, but to the East. But many things get found where you believe they are, even if you hunt where nobody else would.*

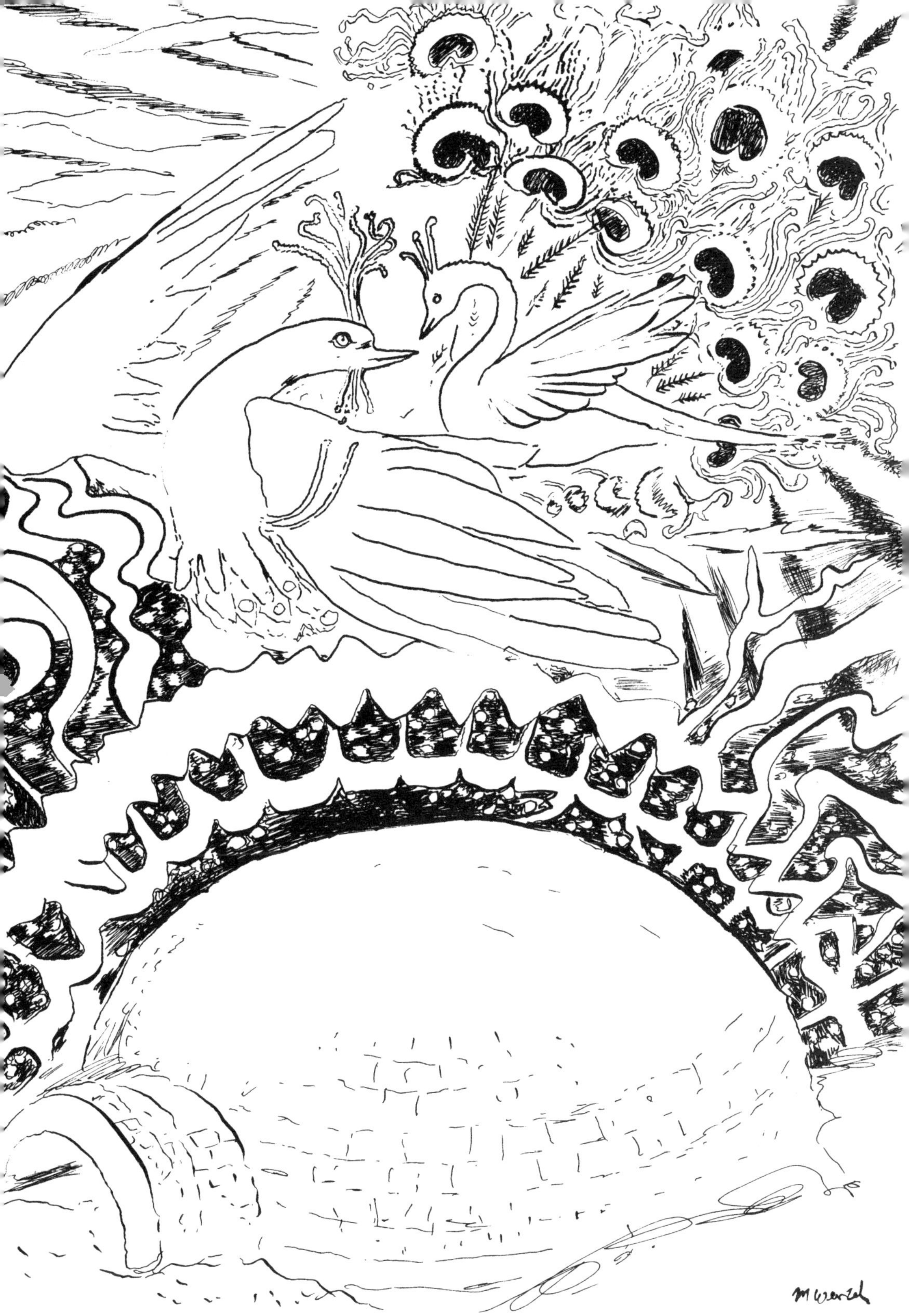

# 24 • The Rabbit and Being Sad

This is a forest story about some animals that wanted to put on a play. All the animals wanted to please the people who watched them act. Pleasing people was their first thought. But the play was going to be about love and death. That meant, some of the actors, to please people, had to act sad. Had to look sad. Acting sad meant they gave pleasure.

One actor was a rabbit. His face had only one expression. He thought this was no good for looking sad. So he decided to accompany his acting with music. Only he didn't know what sad music was. So he went forth on a quest to find out.

He went forth a certain way and met a boy whistling. He asked the boy to whistle something sad. But the boy said he couldn't. He only whistled when he was happy. There wasn't any sad whistling.

So the rabbit went on. He met a man playing a mouth organ. He asked him to play something sad. The man said, 'Certainly.' There was a good sad song he knew. It was called, "Oh, where are you going, Lord Randall my son." And he played it. But only the words were sad. The tune wasn't sad at all. Since when he was playing he wasn't singing, you couldn't then tell if the song was supposed to be sad.

So the rabbit went on. This time he met a fine lover. The lover wasn't making any music but he looked awfully sad and he was beating his chest saying, 'Oh dear, how could I have been so terrible when I saw her last night?'

This impressed the rabbit. He thought he would introduce rhythm into his sad act. So while he was acting, he drummed with his tail. The whole audience clapped at his drumming! So he decided to forget about acting sad, and to be a rabbit drummer in a cabaret act.

*A story by Alperas.*

*John asked, wasn't Anubis proud of his son writing that story? Anubis said they all heard it, and all were proud, and Asteras was giving Alperas a big hug just then. John asked if Thoth liked it, and Thoth said yes he did, but he saw he would have to teach Alperas something about music.*

*Marian said, children often told stories about what they didn't quite understand. She wrote doll cookbooks when she was a child, and always included "hardening" in the recipes, because she didn't understand why just cooking made things hard.*

*John said Anubis was lucky to have a son like Alperas who could tell these wonderful stories. God only had Jesus, and his stories weren't so good. Marian said that wasn't fair; Jesus' stories were remembered a long time after. She reckoned John wouldn't be able to remember Alperas' words even some decades on. She found she forgot them even a few hours on. But John said he wouldn't forget the interesting details, like the little green men.*

## 25 • Birds and Three Apples

Three apples hung on a big tree that had no other fruit. Because they were all about the same, they imagined the tree liked them equally. The tree did like them equally, but thought one apple more or less hardly affected it. Unfortunately, the two outer apples took to plotting against the middle one. Between them, they decided the middle apple should be got rid of. The two outer apples hung higher on the tree than their middle brother, so they pretended the middle apple could not hear their plots.

Determined to put the central apple out of their sphere, the outer apples decided to enlist the help of birds. They realised birds mainly came to the tree to eat apples. They felt themselves safe, for the middle apple was more ripe. For this they had been jealous of it.

'NO NEED TO PUT LEAVES IN FRONT OF YOUR FACE,' they cried to their brother. 'Be showing your beauty to the world.'

The middle apple nearly burst with pleasure at the attention from his siblings, who on the whole paid no attention to him. He rapidly pushed aside leaves concealing his face. The birds at once made a presence on the tree.

Between the part of the tree where the birds were and the pretty apple was, there was a squirrel. He had heard the plots of the not nice brother apples. He told the birds, 'You are really unwise to eat that apple below. The whole lot of poison spray intended for all the fruit of this tree has gone on to it. I recommend these upper apples. They were out of the way of the spray.'

The birds said, 'Thanks, mate.' And they at once ate the upper apples to their core. But the lower apple got eaten by a boy. And the tree was proud he chose it, because he was the son of the man who owned the orchard.

*A story by Alperas, who says, you never know what anyone's motives are. Plotting can be pretty insignificant in the face of the Big Plan of Life.*

*September 29, 1989*
*Marian and John emptied the wheelbarrow, and found in it a lot of snails. Marian put them in a brown plastic box, but they disappeared. Alperas explained this with a story:*

## 26 • The Snail and the Big Hand

Once there was a snail whose home got thrown away. A big hand came and put him in a brown plastic box. He said, 'I'm no sucker, I have suckers, and I can get out of this.' He climbed up one side and down the other side and away, off into the garden.
Then suddenly an enormous hand came down out of the sky and picked up the whole garden and house and everything in it and put it into another box. The box was called life.

*A story by Alperas.*

♥♥♥♥♥♥♥

*Alperas explained, the story meant no road doesn't go somewhere. Doing no more than that which presents itself for a snail to do, may also be rolling the boulders away in front of the action of God. Alperas believes in God, who is a friend of his father's, and says God is always active, particularly where you are.*

LIFE

## 27 • The Soap Bubble that Thought

Going to be almost anything is better than going to be a soap bubble.
This is what the soap bubble thought who thought. Being best on the part of the soap bubble took a lot of energy on the part of the blower, but nothing on the part of the soap bubble except accepting destiny. Both talent and being clever didn't have much to do with events.

This story is about a soap bubble who made the best of being one. He lived in a noble bowl initially, painted with a band of pigs in gold. The bowl got cracked in an earthquake, and given to the children for their tree-house. The bowl was used for the water and soap to make soap bubbles.

One day the soap bubble got made. Being blown forth from a treehouse, high already in the air, the bubble was glorious in both position and size. The kind wind carried him right up in the direction of the clouds. Bright sunlight moved over his surface, breaking the natural soap bubble shimmer with the magnificent reflection of the sun.

Bold of nature, the soap bubble allowed himself thought. His first thought was, he had not much time to make much of his existence. But his second thought was, he had NO TIME TO WASTE. He had time only to sing a song to his beautiful life. That way he was sounding as happy as he should have been. Because to be a soap bubble was to enrich the world like being a field flower. But few field flowers got looked at and admired through their whole lives. The soap bubble did. All the children watched him, and marvelled at him, until he turned into the blue sky itself.

*A story by Alperas.*

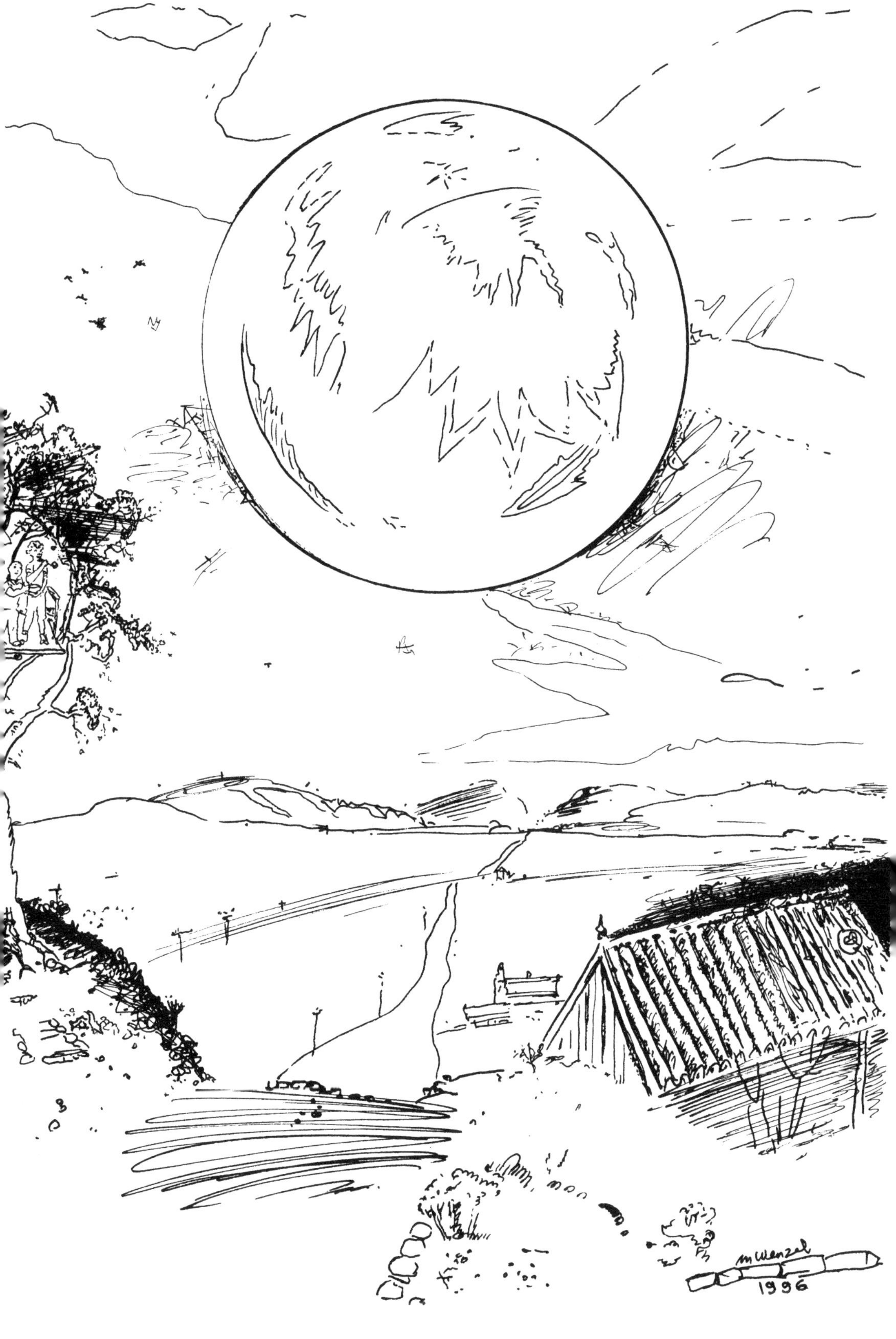
M Wenzel
1996

*November 11, 1990*

*There was a story hovering around one day, waiting to be told, Alperas said. It was the story of not ever being afraid.*

## 28 • The Horse and Not Being Afraid

The story is told to you by Alperas, who hopes he doesn't scare you because you would be afraid then, and you aren't to be. It is about a horse. He lived a long time ago. Books tell about his master, who had a lot of success killing people. One day the horse tired of this. He lots of times thought how he could get away. All the time he was looked after by attendants. So he decided what he would do was, he would make use of a certain boy who worked for his master. The boy loved the horse. The horse decided he would let the boy get ideas he could have his own horse — this one — and build up his own court of people not liking killing.

    Doting on the horse, the boy had the job to exercise him. At a time both knew about, horse and boy ran away. They had no place to go, however. So they let God lead them. God led them to where no war ever came. No privation hollowed their cheeks. No new real trial ever came to them. The place was not book recorded. It hated being known to anyone but them. It had the luck to be such a place successfully. It was nearly a bottomless pit of safety. It was the whole world anywhere. Because both horse and boy lost their ability to be afraid ever again. Their mother and relatives all came too. So did Marian and John, open-eyed with amazement.

    Then they were never frightened again.

*A story by Alperas.*

*Thoth had a celebration one weekend, and Alperas directed Marian and John to Oxfam to buy him a specially selected gift. This was a curved Victorian brush which cost 40p. Written on it were the words: "Fortescue, Notting Hill Gate". Alperas gave a long speech about how the brush and its inscription were symbolic. "Fortescue" meant "Fortitude". "Notting" meant nothing bad, of course. "Hill" meant the hill John and Marian climbed but were about at the top of it and "Gate" meant the gate everybody was going to go through for everything nice always. Dogs had chewed the both ends of the brush making it an appropriate gift from jackals.*

*The first nice thing was the special apple cake John had made, and everyone had some of that. Apis came to bellow a laud in praise of Thoth.*

*Alperas then told a story in honour of the occasion.*

## 29 • Chance and the staple

When the new row of staples was set in to the staple gun, one of the staples was named Harry, and he was known to be very brave. Harry in fact pretended to be brave, but was not. He mortally feared life.

At unexpected times through each day, an unknown force struck a blow at the neck of a member of his regiment, so that it was struck away from the position of safety within the regiment. Getting used to this nerve-wracking situation was hard for Harry to do. He feared the unknown. To be so cowardly, however, was NOT appetising to his heroic spirit.

One day great events occurred. The staples in front of him fell away into the unknown, and Harry had the honour to be in front of the row of potential staple soldier victims. Great pride, but as well terror, filled his breast.

THEN THE PENDULUM OF FATE BURST ITS FATAL BEAT, severing the staples' security and pressing him into new service the nature of which could only be distant from his mind. But this put him in a position of great glory.

The staple fastened a first prize blue ribbon to the winning bull in an animal show. Before him, an entire arena of people cheered and a tall man, who had removed his top hat as symbol of reverence, led him around the arena, where his tight fastening of the blue ribbon raised a vast cheer. Grasping the blue satin with the pride of his race, the staple said, "Life was worth everything."

*A story by Alperas.*

## Summary and Postscript

Marian and John lived in a house on Worcester Shrub Hill. They both worked freelance which means, you never know for sure if you find work. Both worried most of the time, which stopped them from enjoying life and each other. Then Alperas, son of Anubis, came and taught them never again to be afraid.

After these stories were written, Marian and John split up. But they never again **were** afraid. If they ever came in danger of it, they re-read a lost early version of the story, Chance and the Staple, which had been mislaid for a long time, but was then found.

## 30 • Chance and the Staple: preliminary composition

A little staple lived in a staple gun. Ahead of him there was a whole line of family members, so close to each other, that they looked just like a single unit. But they had the toll exacted of them, that they had to be released from each other, and go out into the world doing heavy work all on their own. Each staple knew there was little chance they would be next to a brother or sister after that dramatic moment when a big hand pushed down on the staple gun and they popped downwards, like a parachutist, each landing they did not quite know where, their sturdy legs piercing alien material and joining parts of it together as one.

The staple who was hero of this story, was about two-thirds of the way along the stream of united staples that had been inserted as a family unit into one particular staple gun. The little staple was afraid to let the others know he was afraid, but he was. He knew being used for his destined purpose was quite inevitable. He knew there was little chance his destiny would differ from that of other staples. He knew they had the job of holding pieces of paper together, because the first staple in the stream reported rapidly that what was taking place, and most of the others who got a chance to cry backwards the tale of their transferal of labour of future necessity all reported something the same.

The staple waited in trepidation. Each few days one, sometimes more, of his family disappeared. The lengthy stream of staples, originally so long it seemed never-ending, kept reducing in size, and his position kept changing so it was nearer and nearer the front.

He had only one staple ahead of him, when he decided to rebel. There were moments he had noticed, when staples didn't work. The giant hand pressing the lever at the top of the gun seemed annoyed. The staple clearly hadn't held. Another staple was at once ejected to take its place. The little staple decided he would choose to be a staple that didn't hold. Then he would be freed of future work. He would just be thrown aside and could end living. That was what he thought.

    His turn came. The big hand descended and he let himself be ejected with a loud pop. The determination he had not to work fled. He found he held by both legs a lovely blue ribbon on to a bark basket containing a huge blooming flower the colour of the sun. The ribbon had a golden message written on it. It said FIRST PRIZE. The staple found all sorts of people were coming and peering at him holding his message which made everyone who read it, pleased. He found his life much more interesting than ever before. Than ever he could have imagined on the basis of his experiences just being one little staple in a row of others exactly like himself. There were no other first prize flowers in his group. The staple saw he was unique, and he liked this. Remembrance of family far removed itself from his thoughts.

    Then he noticed other plants had stapled messages. There were things like Best Tall Dahlia. Best Hybrid. That sort of thing. There was companionship among these staples of a sort. He let himself be of their group in a way. But he knew he was out of their group. He was lone, but he was the best. So he never felt fearful again.

*A STORY BY ALPERAS...*

# Contents

| | | |
|---|---|---|
| Introduction | 5 | |
| *This Alperas writes to John* | 6 | |
| 1. Baldwin the Coot and a Little Green Man | 8 | |
| 2. A Christmas Story from Alperas to John | 10 | |
| 3. Mermaids, Green Men and Jackson the Seal | 12 | |
| 4. Miss Brody and the Dragon | 12 | |
| 5. Three Frogs | 14 | |
| *Thoth's Birthday Events* | | |
| 6. The Seven Flies | 16 | |
| 7. The Jackal-headed Boy and Superman | 16 | |
| 8. The Two Mud-puddles | 18 | |
| 9. Two Scouts and a Snake | 18 | |
| 10. The Boy Scouts that were Green Men | 19 | |
| 11. The Scouts and the Birds | 20 | |
| 12. Alperas' Wonderful Story of the Week | 20 | |
| 13. The Firecracker | 23 | |
| *Birth of a Stella Sothis* | 24 | |
| 14. The Little Sting-ray | 24 | |
| 15. The Boy at School | 26 | |
| 16. Flight of the Coots | 26 | |
| 17. Coots on Noah's Ark | 27 | |
| 18. The Crocus that Angered Birds | 28 | |
| 19. The Ladybird and the Flower | 30 | |
| 20. Ibis Humour | 32 | |
| 21. Two Squirrels | 32 | |
| *Alperas stories and the Anubis News* | 33 | |
| 22. Prepare to Meet Thy Poppy | 33 | |
| 23. Peacock Igloo Pie | 34 | |
| 24. The Rabbit and Being Sad | 36 | |
| 25. Birds and Three Apples | 37 | |
| 26. The Snail and the Big Hand | 38 | |
| 27. The Soap Bubble that Thought | 40 | |
| 28. The Horse and Not Being Afraid | 42 | |
| 29. Chance and the Staple | 43 | |
| *Summary and Postscript* | 44 | |
| 30. Chance and the Postscript, Preliminary Composition | 44 | |

# List of Illustrations

| | | |
|---|---|---|
| 1. Alperas Writing Stories | 7 | |
| 2. Baldwin the Coot and a Little Green Man | 9 | |
| 3. Alperas with Inferior Stories He Has Ripped up | 11 | |
| 4. Miss Brody and the Dragon | 13 | |
| 5. Alperas pretending to be Thoth | 15 | |
| 6. The Jackal-headed Boy and Superman | 17 | |
| 7. The Baby Firebird | 21 | |
| 8. The Little Sting-ray | 25 | |
| 9. The Crocus that Angered Birds | 29 | |
| 10. The Ladybird and the Hyacinth | 31 | |
| 11. The Peacock Igloo | 35 | |
| 12. The Snail and the Big Hand | 39 | |
| 13. The Soap Bubble that Thought | 41 | |